JUMP ON BOARD THE ANIMAL TRAIN!

By Naomi Kefford
and Lynne Moore

Illustrated by

Benji Davies

SIMON AND SCHUSTER
London   New York   Sydney   Toronto   New Delhi

It's a special day out for Mummy and me.
There's lots to do and so much to see.

Hold Mummy's hand.
Walk on the wall.

Play with a beetle
down on the ground

Ssh! Listen!
What can it be?

I think there's something following me!

We climb up the hill, my mummy and me.
There's lots to do and so much to see.

Swing on a post.
Round and round.

PARK

TRAINS

CAFÉ

The tiger's tail swishes the rail.
The bear's paws pad on the floor.

And they follow us as we go . . .

We walk on and on, my mummy and me.
There's lots to do and so much to see.

Pick up a stick.
Dig in the mud.

UNDER
CONSTRUCTION.
KEEP OUT

Stamp with my feet.
THUD, THUD, THUD.

Ssh! Listen!
What can it be?

I think there's something following me!

We stop for an ice cream, my mummy and me.
There's lots to do and so much to see.

Shuffle my shoes.
Look at my feet.

Climb on a bench.
Sit on the seat.

Ssh! Listen!
What can it be?

I think there's something following me!

We arrive at the station, a train's drawing near.

The headlights are shining.
Hooray! It's here.

Dad

Ooh! Look!

What can you see?

I can see someone waving at me!

We enter the carriage.
Daddy covers my eyes.

"Are you ready," he asks,
"for a SPECIAL surprise?"

Ssh! Listen! What can it be?
I'm so excited. I can't wait to see . . .